D1316490

randomhousekids.com

ISBN 978-1-5247-6392-3 (trade) — ISBN 978-1-5247-6393-0 (ebook)

Printed in the United States of America

10 9 8 7 6 5 4 3 2 1

The Night ⟨Before⟩ PEEPSmas

By Andrea Posner-Sanchez and Fran Posner
Illustrated by Julissa Mora

 A GOLDEN BOOK · NEW YORK

'Twas the night before PEEPSmas, and all over town
Peeps were preparing both upstairs and down.
They put plants in the windows and wreaths on the doors.
Festive colors soon covered the walls, chairs, and floors.

The tree looked so beautiful with its lights all aglow,
And each ornament hanging from a tiny red bow.

In the kitchen, Peeps hurried this way and that,
Making snacks for everyone—even their cat.

They mixed and they baked—oh, these Peeps did it all.
They made so many treats, some big and some small:

Gingerbread! Candy canes! Peppermint stars!
Sugar cookies! Fruitcakes! And sweet chocolate bars!

The treats smelled so good–
and tasted delicious.

They packed some up and placed
others on dishes.

Then Peeps hung their stockings on the mantel just so
And set out a mat for Santa Peep below.

When darkness fell, they were all nestled in bed,
Dreaming of the sweet surprises ahead.

The night was crisp, the sky crystal clear.
Conditions were right for Santa Peep to appear.
Seated in the back of his magical sleigh,
Eight reindeer with antlers were leading the way.
They zipped and they zoomed as their sled flew around,
Then landed on the roof without making a sound.

The reindeer were happy to rest for a while.

They glanced at Santa Peep, who wore a big smile.

He took his sack with toys and gifts all tucked inside,
Then climbed into the chimney, and down he did slide.

Santa Peep's tummy grumbled as he sniffed the air.
Were there cookies for him over there by the chair?
Yes! Santa Peep sat for his homemade treat.
He loved having something special to eat!

The cookies were yummy. He was hungry no more.
So he went right to work spreading gifts on the floor.
From his sack he pulled storybooks filled with rhymes,
A curly-haired doll, a cuckoo clock that chimes.
Plus paintbrushes, crayons, and bright building blocks,
Stuffed bears, ice skates, and warm, colorful socks.

And inside the stockings he placed more toys,
Carefully, gently, without making noise.

Then up the chimney he went in a dash,
Called to his reindeer, and left in a flash.
There were more homes to visit; he wasn't yet done.
It was a long, busy night, but always great fun.

This is Santa Peep's favorite time of year,
Delivering happiness, gifts, and good cheer!